GAME DAY

Tiki and Ronde Barber with Robert Burleigh

Illustrated by Barry Root

SCHOLASTIC INC.
New York Toronto London Auckland Sydney
Mexico City New Delhi Hong Kong Buenos Aires

For AJ and Chason, again—T. B.

To my three Roses—R. B.

To Ryan Roberts, with love—B. B.

To JMR, SBR, BTR, and KBR, with lots of L—B. R.

ACKNOWLEDGMENTS

Thanks to Brandon Fortna (who served as my model for Ronde and
Tiki) and to Chuck Stephens and Solanco Midget Football.—B. R.

The authors and publisher gratefully acknowledge the assistance
of Mark Lepselter in making this book.

ISBN 0-439-89915-X

Text copyright © 2005 by Tiki Barber and Ronde Barber.
Illustrations copyright © 2005 by Barry Root.
All rights reserved. Published by Scholastic Inc., 557 Broadway, New York, NY 10012,
by arrangement with Simon & Schuster Books for Young Readers,
Simon & Schuster Children's Publishing Division. SCHOLASTIC and
associated logos are trademarks and/or registered trademarks of Scholastic Inc.

12 11 10 9 8 7 6 5 4 3 2 1   6 7 8 9 10 11/0

Printed in the U.S.A.   40

This edition first printing, September 2006

Book design by Einav Aviram
The text for this book is set in Meridien.
The illustrations for this book are rendered in watercolor and gouache.

It was the play Coach Mike liked to call "Old Bread and Butter." Tiki and Ronde knew it by heart.

It went like this: The quarterback took the snap and looked left as both ends broke to their left. Then, with a quick spin, the quarterback pitched the ball back to Tiki, who followed his brother to the opposite side. From there—if everything clicked—it was off to the races.

And this time everything *did* click. The defensive end ran toward the quarter-back. Staying behind Ronde, Tiki sprinted into the clear. The goal line was sixty yards away. At the twenty-yard line, two defensive backs closed in on Tiki. Ronde, leading the way, dove at the knees of the first defender and bounced into the second as all three players went down. Tiki leaped high and kept on going.

Touchdown, Vikings!

"Tiki Barber, number twenty-two, scores!" the announcer called out.

Ronde saw his whole team converge on the end zone, and he sat up and made his way to the milling crowd. He was limping a little. The block he had thrown had somehow hurt his ankle.

"Tiki! Tiki!" All the Vikings crowded around Tiki and cheered. Even some parents had come out onto the field.

Ronde saw his mother looking at Tiki and waving.

He wondered, *If I hadn't made that block, Tiki wouldn't have scored. Didn't anyone notice that I . . . ?*

Coach Mike came up beside Ronde and patted him on the shoulder. "Nice game," the coach said. Then he added, "That twin brother of yours—he's amazing. That's his seventh long touchdown run this season."

"Yeah," Ronde said, his head down.

"You okay?" the coach asked.

"Yeah, I'm okay," Ronde said in a quiet voice. He didn't feel like talking to anyone as he hobbled across the field.

It was Tuesday afternoon, and the twins were in their room doing homework. Ronde suddenly looked up from his book and said, "Guess how long it took Lewis and Clark to go from the Mississippi River to the Pacific Ocean."

"Dunno," Tiki said. "A couple weeks?"

"A couple weeks? It took almost two years!" Ronde grinned. "That's what you know!"

"Well, if two guys row all day . . ."

"It wasn't just two," Ronde answered. "No way." He pointed to his book. "It took almost forty to get there. A whole bunch."

The twins' mother popped her head into the room. "Surprise," she whispered. "Someone's here to talk with you."

A reporter with the Roanoke newspaper was doing a feature story about the city's Pee Wee League. There was a photographer with him too.

"Are you Tiki?" the reporter asked, looking down at Ronde.

Ronde shook his head. "Uh-uh." He pointed at his twin brother.

The reporter turned to Tiki and said, "Your coach tells me you've already scored seven touchdowns in four games. What's your secret?"

Tiki, like Ronde, felt funny talking to adults. He pawed the floor with one foot. Then, in a low voice, he said, "I—I just keep on running. I do my best and the game happens around me."

The reporter went on talking to Tiki. "Those are some long runs—sixty, seventy yards. Don't you get out of breath?"

"Sometimes." Tiki smiled shyly. "But I keep running."

The reporter turned to the photographer. "Let's take his picture outside— holding a football."

They turned to go outside, while Ronde stayed behind. Then the boys' mother called out, "How about taking both boys' picture—together? They're a team. Ronde is Tiki's best blocker."

"Sure," said the reporter. "Great idea."

Later, as the boys' mother cooked dinner, Ronde mumbled in a soft voice to her, "Guys who block and stuff like that—nobody notices. People just notice the guy who scores touchdowns."

His mother was silent for a moment.

Ronde went on. "I'm fast too. At the tryouts this fall I was as fast as Tiki. Why don't I carry the ball more?"

His mother seemed to be thinking. "Hmmmm." Then she popped a funny question: "Who cooks dinners here?"

Ronde looked up. *Why is Mom talking about dinner now?* "You do," he answered.

"And if I were to stop?" his mother asked.

Ronde made a face and thought, *We'd probably be eating peanut butter all the time.*

But before he could say that, his mother jumped in with an answer: "I'll tell you. We'd all starve. And who carries out the garbage each night?"

"Me and Tiki."

"Right on, buster. And if you guys didn't?"

Ronde smiled.

"We'd all have to walk around like this," his mom said as she pinched her nose. She laughed. "It's a good thing we work together here, isn't it?"

Saturday arrived—but Ronde's ankle was still slightly swollen. He sat on the bench in his street clothes, next to Coach Mike. "Can't I maybe play a little—in the second half?" he pleaded.

"No way, José," the coach said firmly. "Besides, next week's game is the big one. Let's get you ready for that."

Tiki trotted over to the bench, out of breath from pregame warm-ups. "Hey," Coach Mike said, laughing and pointing to Ronde, "let's win one for your brother here!"

The Vikings crowded around the coach and Ronde. "Yeah, yeah!" they yelled. Tiki and Ronde gave each other a high five. Tiki said, "Rest up. We really need you next week. Today I'm going to break a couple of long ones for you, Ronde. Watch me."

Yet . . . easier said than done. Again and again, Tiki cut through the line or dodged a slow-footed lineman—only to find himself trapped by two or three defensive backs who hemmed him in and drove him out of bounds. A few times Ronde leaped to his feet and called out, "Go, Tiki, go!" But it didn't do any good.

"Cheering helps," Coach Mike said, "but not as much as a few solid blocks." Then he added softly, "He's missing his main man."

Ronde looked over at his coach, wondering: *Is Coach Mike talking about me?*

The game was tied after three quarters. Finally in the fourth quarter the Vikings slowly ground their way to the winning touchdown. But where were Tiki's long gainers? Not today, not today.

It was the following Wednesday—practice day before their game with the toughest team in the league, the Knights. Ronde felt like a colt who had been let out of the barn. He hopped up and down to test his ankle. He led the team in the warm-up run around the track. He loved the breeze on his face and the feel of the cinders under his shoes.

Coach Mike told Ronde and Tiki to take turns catching and returning punts. As Tiki watched from the bench, Ronde caught ten high, spiraling punts in a row without dropping one, and after each catch he zigzagged and sprinted downfield for twenty yards and then came back. When it was Tiki's turn, Ronde went to the sidelines.

Paco, Ronde and Tiki's best friend, jogged over to where Ronde was sitting. Paco was heavier than the twins, and slower. He played on the offensive line and was a solid blocker.

"Yo, Rond."

"Hey, Pac."

Paco sat down next to Ronde, breathing heavily. "Hitting those blocking dummies is hard work," he said.

Ronde looked at Paco. "Pac, you ever get tired of just blocking for other guys?"

"Sometimes. But I figure someone's gotta do it. And when I do it okay, it feels good. And when we win, it feels really good."

"Yeah."

"I wish I could run fast like you and Tiki, but I can't. So . . ."

Ronde and Paco were quiet for a moment.

Paco went on, "My dad always says this funny thing. He says 'You gotta play your best with the cards you are dealt.' You know, like—"

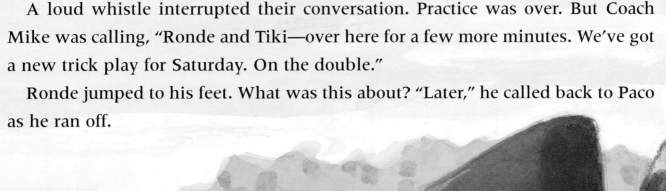

A loud whistle interrupted their conversation. Practice was over. But Coach Mike was calling, "Ronde and Tiki—over here for a few more minutes. We've got a new trick play for Saturday. On the double."

Ronde jumped to his feet. What was this about? "Later," he called back to Paco as he ran off.

Saturday was overcast. The wind swirled and died down and swirled again. The Knights were wearing shiny black uniforms. The gray sky seemed to make the players look even bigger.

Parents stood behind the Vikings' bench and filled the bleachers. Ronde looked over and spotted his mother. She smiled, gave him a thumbs-up, and mouthed the words she always used: *Play proud*. The Vikings gathered around Coach Mike, then jogged onto the field. The boys were psyched up as the start of the game neared.

The game was expected to be close, and at halftime it was tied. Only once—late in the third quarter—did Tiki, behind a great block from his brother, break away for a long touchdown run. But the Knights' bigger size began to show. Slowly, yard by yard, they drove to a touchdown and then edged ahead.

What now?

The Vikings were on their own forty-yard line. It was starting to drizzle, and the clock was running down. The Vikings' blue uniforms were smeared with dirt. Ronde sprinted to the sidelines, listened to the coach, and then raced back. He ducked into the huddle to announce the play. "Coach Mike says"—he looked at Tiki—"it's time for 'Old Bread and Butter Plus One.' "

Jason, the quarterback, glanced up. "Huh," he mumbled. "What's the 'plus one'?"

Tiki broke in: "Don't worry. It's the same old play—with something added."

"Let's do it!" Paco called out as the team headed for the line of scrimmage.

Jason took the snap. He faked a pass to the left and wheeled around. He shoveled the football back to Tiki, who veered outside the onrushing end. Tiki threaded his way downfield, behind his brother, but three defensive backs were closing in.

Then something strange happened. Ronde seemed to miss his block and slide sideways past the defenders. The three tacklers, sure of themselves now, headed for Tiki. It seemed like it was all over. . . .

In a split second Tiki leaped into the air and spun around. With all his strength he lobbed a cross-field lateral pass to Ronde. The football wobbled and dipped.

But Ronde, without breaking stride, bent forward and snatched it cleanly just above his shoes. He tucked the football under his arm and was off.

Ronde ran, faster and faster, with his eyes on the goalposts. The thirty-yard line, the twenty, the ten—

"Touchdown, Ronde Barber!" the announcer called out in a loud voice. "The Vikings win, twenty to fifteen!"

Ronde stood in the end zone and looked back. The whole team was racing downfield toward him. Tiki was there first. Together he and Ronde held the ball high in the air. The Vikings gathered around. Many hands reached in to touch the winning football.

"You did it!" Tiki shouted at Ronde.

Ronde laughed. "No, bro, *you* did it." Then he stopped. "No, we *both* did it." Then he stopped himself again. "No, we *all* did it. Hooray, Vikings!"